W9-BOM-227

ALSO IN THE SERIES

Max Finder Mystery Collected Casebook, Volume 1
2007 Winner for Graphic Novel,
The Association of Educational Publishers'
Distinguished Achievement Award

Max Finder Mystery Collected Casebook, Volume 2
2008 Winner for Graphic Novel,
The Association of Educational Publishers'
Distinguished Achievement Award

Max Finder Mystery Collected Casebook, Volume 3
2008 Finalist for Graphic Novel,
The Association of Educational Publishers'
Distinguished Achievement Award

Max Finder Mystery Collected Casebook, Volume 4

Max Finder Mystery Collected Casebook, Volume 5

Max Finder

MYSTERY

Collected Casebook

Volume 6

10 Lower Spadina Avenue, Suite 400, Toronto, Ontario M5V 2Z2
www.owlkids.com

Distributed in Canada by University of Toronto Press
5201 Dufferin Street, Toronto, Ontario M3H 5T8

Distributed in the United States by Publishers Group West
1700 Fourth Street, Berkeley, California 94710

Library and Archives Canada Cataloguing in Publication

O'Donnell, Liam, 1970-
Max Finder mystery : collected casebook / Liam O'Donnell, Michael Cho.

Vol. 6 by Craig Battle and Ramón Pérez.
Vol. 5-6 issued also in electronic format.
ISBN 978-1-926973-22-7 (bound : v. 6).--ISBN 978-1-926973-21-0 (pbk. : v. 6)

1. Detective and mystery comic books, strips, etc. 2. Mystery games.
I. Cho, Michael II. Battle, Craig, 1980- III. Pérez, Ramón IV. Title.

PN6733.O36M38 2006 j741.5'971 C2006-903300-5

Library of Congress Control Number: 2009935531

Series Design: John Lightfoot/Lightfoot Art & Design Inc.
Design and Art Direction: Barb Kelly

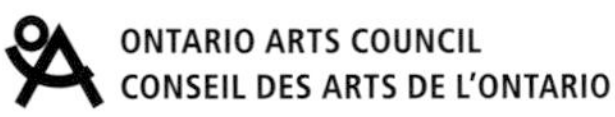

We acknowledge the financial support of the Canada Council for the Arts, the Ontario Arts Council, the Government of Canada through the Canada Book Fund (CBF) and the Government of Ontario through the Ontario Media Development Corporation's Book Initiative for our publishing activities.

Manufactured by WKT Co. Ltd.
Manufactured in Shenzhen, Guangdong, China, in December 2011
Job #11CB2869

A B C D E F

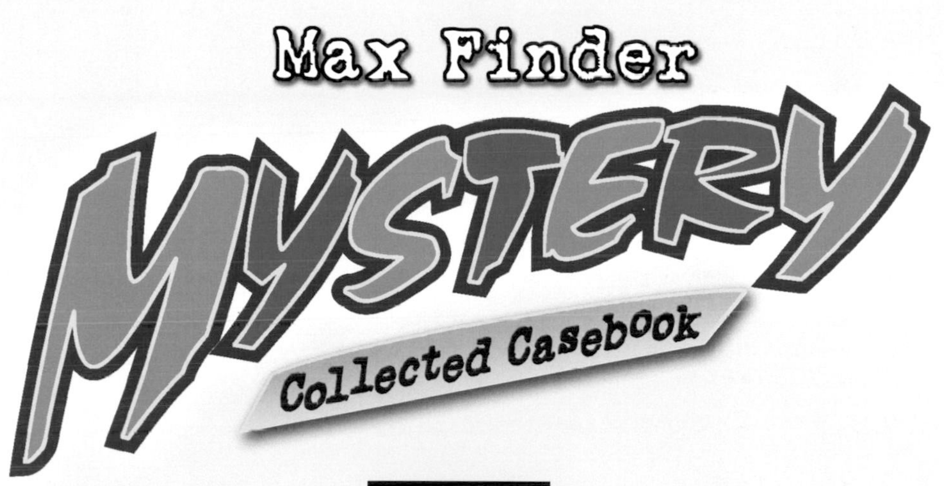

Volume 6

Craig Battle and Ramón Pérez

Created by Liam O'Donnell

Contents

Stories

Extra Stuff

Collected
Casebook
Volume 6

HEY, MYSTERY BUFFS!

Did you know that the book in your hands features a whopping ten comics and two short stories? Max Finder here, fact collector and junior-high detective. In our hometown of Whispering Meadows, my best friend, Alison, and I are the go-to investigators of mysteries big and small. This casebook collects some of our best moments yet.

From the **Green Crime Scene** all the way to the **Daydreaming Detective**, each mystery is crammed with enough clues, suspects, and red herrings to keep you guessing until the end. We've done all the legwork, but solving the mystery is up to you! Read the mysteries, watch for the clues, and try to crack the case. Solutions are at the end of each comic. But remember: real detectives never peek.

So fire up your mystery radar and get solving!

Max

P.S. Check out the lineup on page 11 to get the inside scoop on the characters of Whispering Meadows, and go to page 89 to learn how to host your own mystery party!

TOP SECRET

CHARACTER LINEUP

THE SUSPECTS

Name: Max Finder
Occupation: Detective
Can be found: Studying for the FBI entrance exam or reading spy novels

Name: Alison Santos
Occupation: Journalist & detective
Can be found: Photographing potential crime scenes or playing soccer

Name: Zoe Palgrave
Occupation: Forensics expert
Can be found: Experimenting with her chemistry set

Name: Ben "Basher" McGintley

Occupation: Usual suspect

Can be found: Bullying around town

Name: Ana Guzman

Occupation: New girl in town

Can be found: At her parents' game store

Name: Jake Granger

Occupation: Magician

Can be found: Sneaking up behind Max and Alison

Name: Leslie Chang

Occupation: Gossip

Can be found: Keeping everyone else in line

Name: Dorothy Pafko

Occupation: Co-captain of the Green Thumb Club

Can be found: In the science lab

Name: Stuart DeSilva

Occupation: Gamer

Can be found: In the computer lab

Name: Myron Matthews

Occupation: Aspiring detective

Can be found: Six steps behind Max

Name: Jessica Peeves

Occupation: Local royalty, a.k.a. the mayor's daughter

Can be found: Planning parties

Name: Sasha Price

Occupation: Self-proclaimed local celebrity

Can be found: By the pool

Name: Alex Rodriguez

Occupation: Perfectionist

Can be found: Playing trivia (and winning)

Name: Tony DeMatteo

Occupation: Hockey and football star

Can be found: Hanging out with his older brother

Name: Crystal Diallo

Occupation: Dog walker

Can be found: Reading or drawing manga

THE CASE OF THE...

GREEN CRIME SCENE

THE CASE OF THE... GREEN CRIME SCENE

Max Finder, junior-high detective, here. It was a Wednesday morning in the new school year. Green Thumb Club heads Dorothy Pafko and Jeff Coleman had entered a national video contest to prove we were the greenest school around, and my best friend, Alison, and I were helping out.

We had already filmed segments for our school's cafeteria compost program and the litterless lunch campaign, and now we were outside to check out the school's community garden.

THREE, TWO, ONE... ACTION!

YOU WANT A SCHOOL THAT'S REALLY "GREEN"? HOW ABOUT A SCHOOL THAT GROWS ITS OWN GREENS? COME ON AND...

SHOO!

ANNOYING BIRDS!

CUT!

WHAT A MESS! IT'S GOING TO TAKE DAYS TO CLEAN THIS UP. BY THEN IT MIGHT BE TOO LATE TO SHOOT THE VIDEO!
I CAN SEE TWINDALE DOING THIS TO HURT OUR CHANCES, BUT HOW WOULD THEY KNOW WE HADN'T FILMED THE GARDEN ALREADY?
I DON'T KNOW, DOROTHY. BUT DON'T WORRY. ALISON AND I ARE ON THE CASE.
A few minutes later, our friend and forensic expert, Zoe, showed up to work the crime scene. But not everyone hanging around was on board with her doing her job.
HURRY UP, ZOE. THE CLOCK'S TICKING. I NEED TO GET INTO THE GARDEN TO CLEAN UP.
COOL IT, JEFF! THIS IS A CLOSED CRIME SCENE. PUT THAT EVIDENCE BACK WHERE YOU FOUND IT!

After the crowd dispersed, Zoe took one look at the settled soil and told us the crime must've happened before the previous night's short rain shower, or at about 7:00 or 8:00 p.m.
BUT THERE'S A PROBLEM: THE WOODEN STAKE THAT JEFF TOUCHED HAS GONE MISSING. WITHOUT EVIDENCE, IT'S GOING TO BE A LOT HARDER TO FIGURE OUT WHO DID THIS.

"WHO" OR "WHAT," ZOE? THAT STAKE HAD BITE MARKS ON IT. WE MAY BE LOOKING FOR A K-9 CULPRIT.

Zoe insisted we head to the library right away so she could draw some conclusions from my observations of the bite marks.
BASED ON THE DEPTH AND SIZE OF THE MARKS YOU DESCRIBE, MY GUESS IS THE DOG IN QUESTION IS ONE OF THESE.
COULD BE, ZOE, BUT WE'LL NEED SOME HARDER FACTS IF WE'RE GOING TO CLOSE THIS CASE.
MID-SIZED DOG BREEDS
BULLDOG
BASSET HOUND
MID-SIZED DOG BREEDS
SIBERIAN HUSKY
BORDER COLLIE

What is this, a Max Finder Nemesis Convention? Jake Granger loves two things: 1) magic tricks and 2) competing with me to solve mysteries. Right now, though, it looked like he just wanted to catch his dog.

Jake told us he's terrible with dogs, so his parents make him do dog-walking duty only once a week. Luckily, Crystal Diallo was around to save the day. She has a dog-walking business and is the best handler in town.

After I dusted myself off, we headed back over to the garden, where Jeff was hard at work.

MAX! MY FRIEND FROM TWINDALE'S GREEN TEAM SAID THEY DIDN'T KNOW ABOUT OUR GARDEN, AND SHE FEELS BAD SOMEONE MESSED IT UP. SHE ALSO TOLD ME SOMETHING ELSE.
WHAT'S THAT?

LUKAS HAJDUK IS THEIR CAMERA OPERATOR.
VERY INTERESTING. HE COULD'VE TRASHED THE GARDEN TO HELP TWINDALE WIN THE CONTEST. AND...
BRING

HELLO? ZOE? WHERE ARE YOU?
OVER HERE!

I HAD NO LUCK FINDING CLUES AT THE CRIME SCENE, SO I DECIDED TO WIDEN MY SEARCH AREA. THAT'S WHEN I FOUND THIS. IT LOOKS LIKE A DOG WAS TIED UP HERE AND CHEWED THROUGH THIS LEASH.
I WAS OVER HERE YESTERDAY AFTERNOON. THAT WASN'T THERE!

GOOD FIND, ZOE. THAT LEASH IS THE KEY TO COLLARING OUR CROOK.
THAT'S RIGHT. WE KNOW WHO TRASHED THE COMMUNITY GARDEN.
Do you know who trashed the garden? All the clues are here. Turn the page for the solution.

THE CASE OF THE...
GREEN CRIME SCENE

Who trashed the garden?

Peaches. Crystal tied Peaches up by the field so she could play Capture the Flag, but Peaches chewed through the leash and got into the garden. Crystal felt so bad about it she tried to cover it up.

Clues

- Crystal said she wasn't at the field the night before, but Jake said she was the MVP of the last game of Capture the Flag. She was lying to Max to make herself look innocent.
- The chewed-through leash was the same type that Crystal was using to walk the three dogs. In fact, Max noticed that there was a small price tag still on one of them. Crystal needed to replace the one Peaches ruined the night before.
- Alison noticed that Peaches likes to chase birds. She remembered that earlier in the day, Jeff had to shoo birds out of the garden, which explained why Peaches would go there. Once the birds flew away, Peaches chewed up the garden.
- According to Zoe, both Peaches (a bulldog) and Jake's dog, Max (a Siberian husky), could have made the bite marks on the stake. However, because Jake walks his dog only once a week, he would not have had Max at the field the night the garden was trashed.
- Lukas Hajduk's dog, a Great Dane, is much too large and strong to leave the bite marks of a mid-sized dog.
- Jeff may have been meddling with the crime scene, but he didn't steal any evidence. Crystal was one of the kids at the crime scene in the morning, and she had the stake in her back pocket as she walked away.

Conclusion

Max presented his evidence and Crystal came clean—she felt terrible about Peaches tearing up the garden on her watch. She enlisted everyone from Capture the Flag to help the Green Thumb Club prepare the garden for the video, and Central Meadows went on to win the contest.

THE CASE OF THE...

GHASTLY GHOST WALK

THE CASE OF THE... GHASTLY GHOST WALK

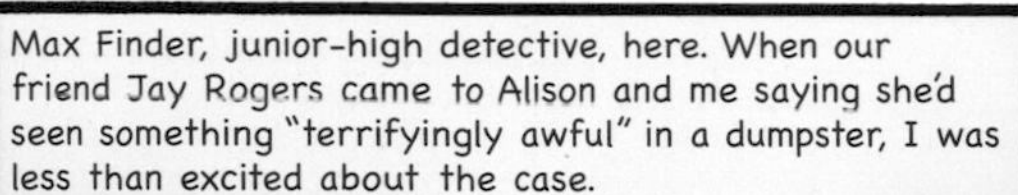

The walk was going great until we got to the alley a few minutes later. The ghost popped out of the dumpster while Annette was talking, and people were not impressed. Especially not Basher McGintley.

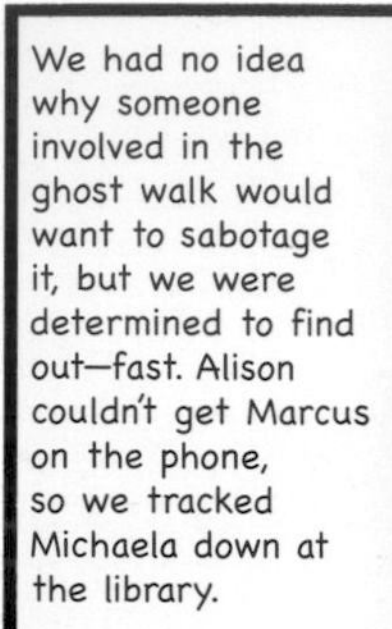
We had no idea why someone involved in the ghost walk would want to sabotage it, but we were determined to find out—fast. Alison couldn't get Marcus on the phone, so we tracked Michaela down at the library.

DO YOU KNOW WHO MIGHT HAVE BEEN BEHIND LAST NIGHT'S SABOTAGE?
PERIODICALS
I CAN THINK OF TWO PEOPLE. THE FIRST IS ANNETTE. SHE WANTED TO DO A SCARY GHOST WALK FROM THE BEGINNING, BUT MARCUS AND I OUTVOTED HER. SHE COULD STILL BE MAD.
THE SECOND IS BRIAN. HE RUNS THE HAUNTED HOUSE IN TOWN AND COULD BENEFIT FROM THE GHOST WALK GOING DOWN.

I BET YOU CAN FIND BOTH OF THEM AT THE INTERNET CAFÉ. BRIAN WORKS THERE AND ANNETTE'S THERE *24/7* VIDEO CHATTING WITH HER BOYFRIEND.
THANKS, MICHAELA. DO YOU HAVE ANY IDEA WHERE WE CAN FIND MARCUS?
HE WAS ACTUALLY RIGHT HERE A SECOND AGO. HE SORT OF TOOK OFF WHEN HE SAW YOU GUYS COMING.

Alison was steamed that Marcus was ducking us, but you know what they say: "The case must go on!" We found Brian at the café and asked him if he knew anything about last night's "ghost."
ONLY 2 DAYS LEFT UNTIL THE HAUNTED HOUSE! BE THERE OR BE SCARED! FOR MORE INFO. CALL CASPER
BRIAN
SORRY, GUYS. A PILLOWCASE GHOST? ANY KID IN TOWN COULD PUT THAT TOGETHER.

WHILE WE'RE HERE, DO YOU MIND TELLING US WHAT YOU WERE DOING LAST NIGHT?
I WAS SCARING KIDS DOWN AT THE HAUNTED HOUSE. YOU GUYS SHOULD CHECK IT OUT.
THE GHOST WALK IS A JOKE!
THAT SOUNDS LIKE ANNETTE...

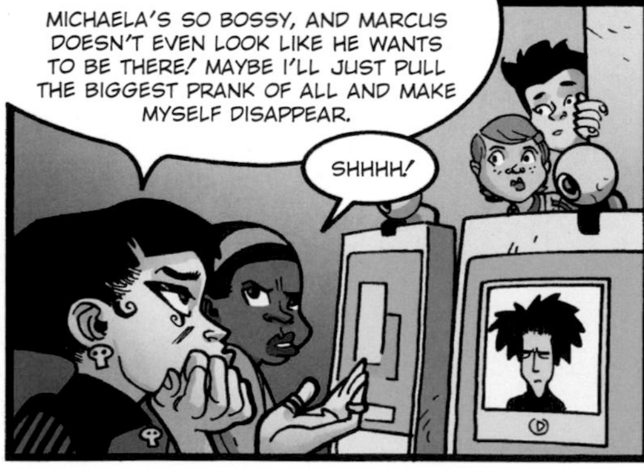
MICHAELA'S SO BOSSY, AND MARCUS DOESN'T EVEN LOOK LIKE HE WANTS TO BE THERE! MAYBE I'LL JUST PULL THE BIGGEST PRANK OF ALL AND MAKE MYSELF DISAPPEAR.
SHHHH!

Did I mention that Jay is a master of disguise? She made me up so I was completely unrecognizable for my ghost walk stakeout. I had just one question about that...

I bought a ticket from Marcus without him recognizing me. Then the walk started and things got interesting...just as we'd hoped.

Do you know who's sabotaging the ghost walk? All the clues are here. Turn the page for the solution.

THE CASE OF THE...
GHASTLY GHOST WALK

Who's messing with the ghost walk?

Brian Casperov. He sabotaged the ghost walk to eliminate competition for his haunted house, which was going to start in two days.

Clues

- Brian told Max that he was scaring kids at the haunted house on the night of the first ghost walk. However, a sign in the internet café said the haunted house hadn't started yet. He was lying.
- Basher said he was hired by someone named Casper. Max noticed that Brian's name tag said his last name was Casperov, and the sign announcing the haunted house said to call "Casper" for more info. Casper is Brian's nickname.
- Michaela said Annette video chats at the internet café all the time, and while Max and Alison were there, she was revealing details about the ghost walk. That explains how Brian would've learned the ghost walk route in order to plan his prank.
- There were a lot of Tenretni Café coffee cups in the dumpster when Max, Jay, and Alison found the pillowcase ghost. That's because the alley is next to the café. That means Brian would have had access to the roof to rig up a pulley system.
- Marcus was ducking Max and Alison because he had something to hide, but it wasn't sabotaging the ghost walk. As Michaela told the crowd, he had a bad case of stage fright and was embarrassed about it.
- Annette may have wanted a more scare-oriented ghost walk, but she didn't commit the crime. According to Jay's testimony, she was talking to the crowd at the time of the prank and wouldn't have been able to pull the rope to lift the lid of the dumpster.

Conclusion

When Max and Alison presented their evidence, Brian emerged from the shadows and confessed. He apologized for trying to sabotage the ghost walk and even offered to split the profits of the haunted house to make up for it. Annette, Michaela, and Marcus finished the ghost walk that night, and everyone walked away impressed—not to mention a little freaked out!

THE CASE OF THE...

GAMING GAFFE

THE CASE OF THE... GAMING GAFFE

A few minutes after the break started, word spread that Whispering Meadows' best pretzel truck was outside, and we all rushed out to get in line.

Stuart DeSilva is our school's biggest techie—he can take apart a computer and put it back together in his sleep. But Coach Sweeny, the organizer of the tournament, had found a problem that even Stuart couldn't solve.
ALL THE GAMES AND DETACHABLE HARD DRIVES HAVE BEEN STOLEN FROM THE GAME SYSTEMS. WITHOUT THEM, WE CAN'T KEEP THE TOURNAMENT GOING.
HEY, GUYS! IT LOOKS LIKE THE THIEF FORGOT ONE SYSTEM. THE HARD DRIVE FOR THIS ONE'S STILL HERE.
THAT'S THE BEST NEWS I'VE HEARD ALL DAY. EVERYONE CAN JUST TAKE TURNS ON THAT ONE. FIRE IT UP, ZOE.

CONGRATS
YOU'VE BEEN HACKED
BY BENT WEATHERS
UH-OH...
CONGRA

Things weren't looking any better when Coach Sweeny reviewed the tournament rule book.
SAYS HERE THAT IN THE CASE OF A STOP IN PLAY DUE TO TECHNICAL DIFFICULTIES, WE HAVE TO AWARD THE TOP PRIZE TO THE ENTRANT WITH THE HIGHEST SCORE. IF WE DON'T FIND THE GAMES SOON, I HAVE TO DECLARE HOLLY THE WINNER OF THE TOURNAMENT.
YOU DON'T HAVE TO DO THAT YET, COACH. WE'LL FIND THE THIEF FOR YOU.

Coach Sweeny agreed to give us an hour to solve the case. But it wasn't going to be easy. We had no witnesses and a lot of potential suspects.
IS IT ME, OR DOES COACH SWEENY SEEM AWFULLY EAGER TO STOP THE TOURNAMENT?
I HEARD HE GOT ROPED INTO ORGANIZING THE EVENT. HE'S ALSO SAID THAT HE DOESN'T THINK VIDEO GAMING IS A SPORT.
HEY, GUYS, I FOUND SOMETHING!

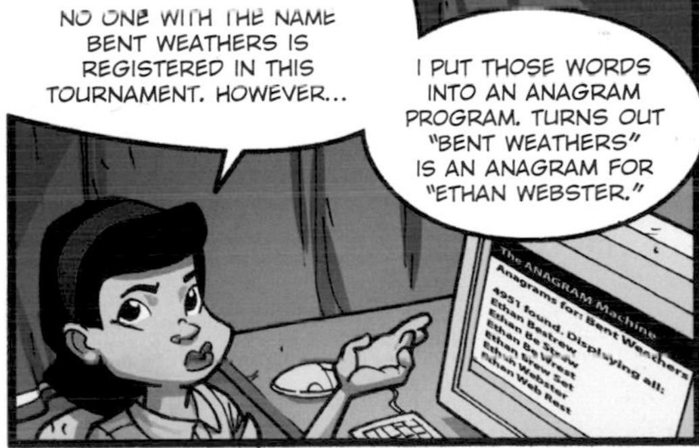
NO ONE WITH THE NAME BENT WEATHERS IS REGISTERED IN THIS TOURNAMENT. HOWEVER...
I PUT THOSE WORDS INTO AN ANAGRAM PROGRAM. TURNS OUT "BENT WEATHERS" IS AN ANAGRAM FOR "ETHAN WEBSTER."
The ANAGRAM Machine

We started looking high and low for Ethan, but he proved hard to spot until...
ETHAN! WAIT!

I THINK HE DUCKED IN HERE, MAX!
COME ON OUT, ETHAN! OR WE'RE COMING IN AFTER YOU!
SUPPLIES
KNOCK KNOCK KNOCK

SLAM
HEY, GUYS! CAN I HELP YOU?

WHAT WOULD YOU SAY IF WE TOLD YOU THE HACKER'S TAG IS AN ANAGRAM FOR YOUR NAME?
I'D SAY IT DOESN'T PROVE ANYTHING! I WORK HERE PART TIME, SO THE THIEF WOULD KNOW I'D BE HERE TO TAKE THE FALL.

Ethan kicked us out to get back to work, so we went to find Holly. But like her buddy Ethan, she wanted nothing to do with us.
MIND IF WE ASK YOU A FEW...
SAVE IT, MAX! I'M NOT THE THIEF. I ENTERED THE TOURNAMENT TO PROVE I COULD PLAY, NOT TO PROVE I COULD WIN BY DEFAULT.

BESIDES, THERE'S A MUCH BETTER SUSPECT IN HERE THAN ME. HE'S BEEN TALKING MORE TRASH THAN SAMIR AND HAS ACCESS TO EVERYTHING. WHY DON'T YOU GO TALK TO STUART DESILVA?

With a little digging, we found out Stuart had wanted to enter the tournament but didn't get his entry form in on time. After that, he decided to volunteer to help out Coach Sweeny.
IT MUST HAVE MADE YOU PRETTY MAD THAT THE TOURNAMENT WOULDN'T MAKE AN EXCEPTION FOR YOU, HUH, STUART?
OF COURSE IT DID! I MEAN...UH, SORT OF. BUT I GOT OVER IT.

YOU WERE THE FIRST TO NOTICE THE GAME SYSTEMS HAD BEEN TAMPERED WITH. WHO ELSE WAS IN HERE WITH YOU?
SAMIR WAS IN THE STANDS EATING A CHOCOLATE BAR, AND COACH SWEENY WAS GLUED TO A MONITOR AT THE ORGANIZER'S TABLE. I'M SURPRISED HE DIDN'T SEE ANYTHING.

A few minutes later, our hour was almost up and Coach Sweeny was ready to throw in the towel.
YOU DID YOUR BEST, GUYS, BUT I THINK THIS IS ONE CASE THAT'S GOING TO REMAIN UNSOLVED. THOSE GAMES AND HARD DRIVES COULD BE ANYWHERE BY NOW.

WHOA! HOLD UP, COACH!
Bent Weathers

WHAT GIVES, ALISON?
ONE PERSON'S TRASH IS ANOTHER PERSON'S CASE-SOLVING CLUE, MAX. I KNOW WHO'S TAMPERING WITH THIS TOURNAMENT.
Do you know who stole the games and hard drives? All the clues are here. Turn the page for the solution.

SOLUTION:

THE CASE OF THE... GAMING GAFFE

Who tampered with the tournament?

Samir Gill. He was angry because he got knocked out of the tournament, so he stole all the games and hard drives to shut it down. He also framed Ethan for the crime.

Clues

- "Bent Weathers" may be an anagram for "Ethan Webster," but when Alison saw the name on the disc, she recognized the handwriting as Samir's. It was an exact match to the writing from the name card Samir was wearing on his back.
- Ethan and Holly were outside in line at the pretzel stand while the crime went down, but Samir wasn't. He used the pretzel distraction to steal the games and hard drives.
- Stuart said Samir had been eating a chocolate bar in the stands shortly after the games and hard drives were stolen. That explains the brown fingerprint Alison saw on the disc—it was chocolate from Samir's hands.
- Coach Sweeny was inside at the time of the crime, as Stuart said, but he was watching a football game on his computer. That's why he didn't notice anything. It's also why he tried to get out of organizing the tournament.

Conclusion

When Alison presented her evidence, Samir confessed. He apologized for being a sore loser and returned the games and hard drives to Coach Sweeny. He had hidden them behind the large curtain at the front of the room, and had dropped his chocolate bar wrapper in front of the curtain when he did. The gaming tournament continued, and Vitamin H wound up winning after all...fair and square!

The Case of the Swimming Pool Stakeout

As told by Alison Santos

3:15: Alison Santos, junior-high detective, here. My friend Zoe asked for my help while Max is out of town visiting his aunt, and that's why I'm hidden underneath the metal bleachers at the side of Whispering Meadows' indoor community pool. The facts on the case: someone in Zoe's swimming class has dumped bright purple food coloring in the pool in each of the last two sessions. The water had to be drained each time, which is a huge waste, and pool officials are threatening to cancel the class if the color dumping doesn't stop.

I'm here to look through the spaces of the bleacher benches, jot down everything that goes on in my trusty notepad, and see if I can catch the culprit red-, or in this case, purple-handed. From my hiding spot I get a great view of everything, from the door of the change rooms at the shallow end of the pool to the diving board at the deep end. I can also see through the wall of windows on the opposite side of the pool.

Class starts in fifteen minutes. I had to get in here before anyone else so I wouldn't be seen. The bad news is it's dirty and steamy under these bleachers. The good news is I've got some awesome stakeout food.

3:18: This just in: cheese puffs are GOOD!

3:20: We have activity at poolside. Alex Rodriguez, our school's resident overachiever, just came out of the change room holding a cell phone.

3:23: Here's what he had to say as he walked around the pool, stopping only once on the other side of the diving board to tie his shoe:

> Mom? Hi, it's Alex. Yes, I'm at swimming class. That's what I need to talk to you about. I need to change classes. Why? Because I can't be in the same swimming class as my little sister! Katlyn is always hanging around me in the pool and always wants to be my partner for stuff. It's embarrassing!
> Uh...hello? Okay. Yes, Mom. Sure. Bye.

3:24: Alex was steaming mad as he hung up the phone. Looks like we have suspect #1. Maybe getting this class canceled is his backup plan if he can't convince his mom to put him in a different one.

3:25: Busy place! Carylin Dell, the class's swimming instructor, just walked from the lifeguard office to the pool deck. She's wearing puffy red nylon shorts over a red one-piece bathing suit and holding a small plastic container and a bottle of purple liquid.

3:26: Ms. Dell just scooped up some water from the pool with the container and squeezed a couple drops of purple liquid into it. She watched the water in the container for a second, smiled, and then walked back to her office. Interesting!

3:27: When Zoe asked me to help her out, she mentioned that Ms. Dell was recently accepted into a national-level swimming club. Rumor has it that she wants more time for training and wishes she didn't have to teach this class. Double interesting!

3:29: Ugh. Too many jujubes...

3:30: Finally! Class is about to start, and it looks like everyone's present. On top of Zoe, Alex, and his little sister, Katlyn, there are the following seven kids: Layne Jennings, Ursula Curtis, Kyle Kressman, Lorrisa Swart, Kate Yoon, Felix Reeves, and Jeff Coleman. All the boys are wearing baggy swim shorts, Layne and Lorrisa are wearing one-piece bathing suits, and Ursula and Kate are wearing suits with board shorts. That means six kids—plus Ms. Dell—could be hiding a bottle of food coloring on them.

3:32: Scratch that! Ms. Dell just asked the entire class to turn out their pockets before jumping in the pool. Kyle and Alex refused at first (Alex mumbled in his deep voice that it was a "violation of personal rights and freedoms"), but everyone did it eventually. Verdict: no food coloring.

3:33: Everybody in the pool!

3:35: Zoe just waved at me. (Note to self: teach her the meaning of the word "incognito.") Luckily, I don't think anyone noticed.

3:41: Early excitement: Kyle just got caught splashing water in Lorrisa's eyes, and Ms. Dell kicked him out of the class. From what Zoe tells me, this happens a lot—Kyle's our school's biggest prankster. Looks like he goes on the suspect list, too. If he sticks around...

3:42: Kyle walked over me on the bleachers to get his towel and dripped pool water all over me. So...GROSS.

3:47: Class has resumed. They're learning the backstroke. Ms. Dell is telling everyone to make sure that their heads are back, their backs are arched, and their toes are down in the water. This is the best swimming class I've ever taken!

3:50: Uh-oh. Junior-high super-bully Basher McGintley just walked by the windows outside. Please tell me he's not coming in here...

3:55: Oh MAN! Not only is Basher in the pool area, but he chose a seat on the bleachers RIGHT ABOVE ME.

3:56: Zoe told me to look out for this: Basher often shows up for the 4:30 free swim, and lately he's been showing up early.

3:58: Enough bashing Basher. On with the stakeout! Ms. Dell asked everyone to partner up, and something very intriguing happened. Here's how it went down:

> Ms. Dell: Okay, class, split off into partners. We're going to swim a quick backstroke relay race.
>
> Katlyn: Alex! Let's be partners! We'll be the best team here!
>
> Felix (mocking Alex): Oooooh, Alex! You're the best!
>
> Jeff: Yeah, Alex. You're the best big brother ever!
>
> Alex: Shut up, you guys. I hate this class!

3:59: Alex's outburst sent Katlyn racing for the change room with tears streaming down her face.

4:01: KATLYN JUST RAN OUT OF THE CHANGE ROOM AND THREW SOMETHING INTO THE POOL! CASE CLOSED?! HAVE I BEEN SITTING UNDER A SET OF BLEACHERS FOR FORTY-FIVE MINUTES FOR NOTHING?!!!

4:02: False alarm. It was just Alex's cell phone, which, of course, will never work again.

4:04: Undaunted, Ms. Dell has gotten Katlyn back in the pool and is still trying to organize the relay race. She paired Alex with Jeff and Felix with Katlyn and told everyone to go hold on to the side of the pool at the deep end.

4:05: Basher's buddies, Dwayne and Shayne, just showed up. They may be big, mean, and nasty (I could go on...), but at least they got Basher talking when they asked him about the food-coloring pranks. Here's what he had to say:

> I got a real good feeling something's going to go down here today, and I'm glad you guys are here to see it. I'm going to document the whole thing.

4:06: Basher just grabbed something from his bag, but I couldn't see what it was.

4:07: The race is about to start, but Basher's legs are BLOCKING MY VIEW!!!

Ms. Dell: Ready, set... go!

4:08: PANDEMONIUM! !!!

4:09: As half the class was churning the pool into a frenzy and Jeff was taking an early lead, Kyle ran up to the windows on the opposite side of the pool and pressed his face against the glass. A deep voice from the deep end yelled "Look!" and everyone stopped racing and turned to look at Kyle. Ms. Dell hopped out of the pool, pointed at him, and shouted at him to go away.

SPLASH! Through Basher's legs I saw a bottle of food coloring fly toward the shallow end and hit the water.

4:10: And... there it is. A growing purple cloud in the water near the middle of the pool. Was that a click I just heard above me?!

4:11: Basher is standing up on the bleachers now, and I have my clear view of the pool area back. Zoe is looking right at me, and it's clear she didn't see who it was either. Someone above me just said, "Nice shot, Basher!"

4:12: Everyone in the pool is looking around, wondering who, if any of them, is the culprit. But Ms. Dell doesn't look like she wants to hang around to find out. She just threw up her arms and said, "All right. Everybody out of the pool. For good!"

For good? I don't think so.

I'm ready to throw in this food-coloring criminal's towel. I may not have seen who threw the bottle, but that doesn't matter. I *know* who did.

Alison

Turn the page for the solution.

THE CASE OF THE... SWIMMING POOL STAKEOUT

Who threw the food coloring?

Alex Rodriguez. He *really* didn't want to be in the same class as his sister.

Clues

- When Alison described her view from under the bleachers, she said there was a diving board by the deep end. She also said Alex stopped behind the diving board to tie his shoe while he was talking to his mom. He planted the food-coloring bottle there while Alison couldn't see him.
- Alison said she saw the bottle of food coloring fly toward the shallow end. That means it must've been thrown from the deep end of the pool, where Alex was. It also means Basher and his buddies couldn't have thrown it.
- Alison said Alex and Jeff were partners in the relay race. Since Jeff was taking an early lead, Alex would've been waiting his turn at the deep end.
- A deep voice called from the water to direct everyone's attention to Kyle's antics. It was Alex using Kyle as a distraction. Earlier, Alison said Alex mumbled in a deep voice about his rights and freedoms.
- Ms. Dell may have been directing attention toward Kyle while he was making faces at the windows, but she didn't throw the food-coloring bottle. According to Alison's notes, Ms. Dell was busy hopping out of the pool while the bottle was being thrown.
- The plastic container and bottle of purple liquid Ms. Dell was holding before class started were used to test the water quality of the pool.
- Zoe said Basher had been showing up early to the free swim. That's how he knew someone had been dumping food coloring in the water. The click Alison heard was Basher taking a photo to "document" the food-coloring cloud and ensuing mayhem.

Conclusion

Alison emerged from under the bleachers to deliver her evidence, and Alex confessed. Ms. Dell kicked him out of the class and, with no more pranks on the horizon, agreed to teach until the end of the year. Basher joined up so he could bridge the time between the end of school and the free swim, and Alison... stayed away from junk food for a while!

THE CASE OF THE...

SUSPICIOUS SET

THE CASE OF THE... SUSPICIOUS SET

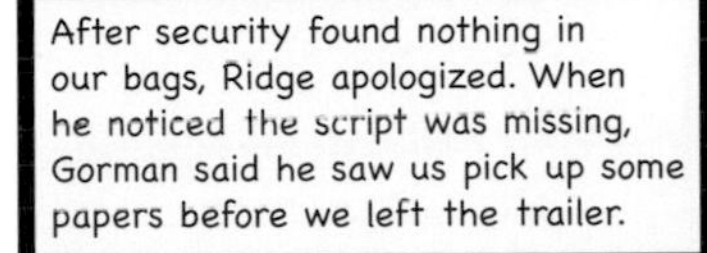

As the lead character in the Dogtown Malone movies, Ridge is one of the toughest guys ever to grace the silver screen. But even he cowered in the face of his producer, Shereece Whimperspoon. He also lied through his teeth.

After Shereece left, Ridge said he had to run interference with other movie people. We went to find Gorman and ask him some questions.

SPIES? DOES HE EXPECT US TO BELIEVE THAT?
I WAS THINKING THE SAME THING. HE COULD JUST BE TRYING TO THROW US OFF THE SCENT.

After that, we bumped into security guard Marge Hudson. While she wasn't happy about working with a couple of kid detectives, she filled us in on what she knew.
WE KEEP A LOG OF ALL MOVEMENT ON THE LOT AT NIGHT. MOST OF THE PEOPLE AROUND RIDGE'S TRAILER WERE REGULARS: ACTORS, THEIR FAMILIES, AND GORMAN.
DID ANYBODY SEE ANYTHING UNUSUAL?

One of our security personnel noted that Gorman was walking with an unidentified person. He had some things to say about Ridge, and they weren't friendly.
RIDGE IS A TOTAL SLAVE DRIVER! I'M STARTING TO THINK I NEVER SHOULD'VE TAKEN THIS JOB!

WHEN THE GUARD CAUGHT UP WITH GORMAN, THE MYSTERY PERSON HAD VANISHED INTO THIN AIR. I DON'T KNOW WHO IT WAS, BUT IT'S DEFINITELY SUSPICIOUS.

EVERYBODY JUST STAY AWAY FROM ME! I HATE THIS STUPID SET!
IS THAT THE STAR OF THE MOVIE?
THAT'S THE STAR'S TEENAGE KID: MARSHMALLOW SWEETEN.

Marge said she needed to chase down some leads before the end of her shift at noon, so we left her and caught up with Marshmallow in the craft services tent.
HEY, WE SAW YOU WALKING ON THE SET JUST NOW. SOUNDS AS IF YOU REALLY DON'T LIKE IT HERE.
WHY WOULD I? IT'S COLD, BORING, AND MY PARENTS WON'T LET ME HANG OUT WITH ANYONE ON SET. THEY THINK SHOW BUSINESS PEOPLE ARE SHALLOW. I'M GOING BONKERS HERE!

WELL, THAT GOT US NOWHERE.
I DON'T KNOW, ALISON. I'D SAY IT GOT US TO THE PERFECT SPOT.
SECUR
GOT QUEST
NEED HELP
CONTACT
SECURITY:
555-465-
SHIFT CHANG
AT NOON &
MIDNIGHT
EVERY DAY.
Special

?
SORRY, MS. WHIMPERSPOON, BUT I LIED TO YOU EARLIER. MY SHOOTING SCRIPT HAS BEEN STOLEN...
THAT'S TRUE, BUT I KNOW WHO STOLE IT. AND THEY'RE STILL ON THE LOT... FOR NOW.
Do you know who stole the shooting script? All the clues are here. Turn the page for the solution.

THE CASE OF THE... SUSPICIOUS SET

Who stole Ridge's shooting script?

Marge Hudson. She was a spy for Furious Films and stole the script to derail production.

Clues

- Gorman said Ridge liked to roll up his shooting script to yell at people through it. Marge had a thick document on her clipboard that was rolling in on itself. It was the script.
- When Max saw the poster showing the security crew for the film, he noticed that Marge's picture was nowhere on it.
- Max also noticed that Marge's hat said "FF" on it. That stands for Furious Films, the name of the underhanded movie studio that Gorman mentioned. The other guards' hats read "SF," for Serious Films.
- Because Marge was wearing the security guard outfit, though, she would've had unlimited access to Ridge's trailer after hours. That's how she stole the shooting script. She was still on the lot waiting to slip out during the security shift change at noon.
- Gorman may have been walking around late at night with a mysterious person, but it wasn't a thief—it was Marshmallow Sweeten. Max realized this when he saw the two passing a note outside the craft services tent. They were sneaking around because Marshmallow's parents won't let her hang out with anyone on set, and she didn't want to get in trouble.

Conclusion

When Max presented his evidence, Ridge and Shereece locked down the set. The real security team got to work and found Marge trying to sneak off. She gave the shooting script back to Ridge and was kicked off the set. Shooting went on as scheduled, and *Ice Planet Okapi* turned out to be the "coolest" movie of the year!

THE CASE OF THE...

GARAGE SABOTAGE

THE CASE OF THE... GARAGE SABOTAGE

We got to the garage by retracing Ursula's steps through the house. I don't know much about amps, but I know a broken one when I hear it.

MAX, CHECK THIS OUT. THE WINDOW OF THE GARAGE DOOR HAS BEEN BUSTED IN. THAT MEANS SOMEONE OUTSIDE THE GARAGE DID THE BREAKING.

THAT'S USUALLY A SIGN OF FORCED ENTRY, BUT THE WINDOW FRAME ITSELF DOESN'T SEEM LARGE ENOUGH FOR SOMEONE TO FIT THROUGH. THE CULPRIT ALSO COULDN'T REACH THE SIDE DOOR FROM THERE TO UNLOCK IT.

DO YOU THINK MAYBE URSULA BLEW OUT THE AMP ON HER OWN AND IS LOOKING FOR A SCAPEGOAT TO PIN IT ON?

While I was covering our tracks, Alison was uncovering a clue. She found a hockey ball with the letters "KY" written on it.

Andy is Ursula's older brother. He goes to high school in Twindale, taking a long bus ride there and back every day. He didn't seem too upset about the amp when Ursula told him about it.

While we played, Kate told us her first shot of the afternoon went up over the net and through Ursula's garage window.

After we finished with Kate, we knocked on Drew Bacca's door. He goes to our school and plays drums in Ursula's band. We filled him in on the case, and he seemed really angry about the amp.

WHAT WERE YOU DOING THIS AFTERNOON? KATE SAID SHE SAW YOU OVER BY THE GARAGE EARLIER.

I WENT OVER TO URSULA'S TO GRAB MY DRUMSTICKS, BUT NO ONE WAS HOME. THAT'S WHEN I SAW KATE. SHE JUST YELLED SOMETHING AT ME AND TOOK OFF IN A HURRY.

THE CASE OF THE...
GARAGE SABOTAGE

Who blew out Ursula's amp?

Drew Bacca. He wanted to play guitar, so he used Ursula's family's set of emergency keys to get into the garage, but he accidentally blew out the amp in the process.

Clues

- Ursula said her drummer, Drew, wants to play guitar. That explains why he was fiddling with the guitar and amp in the first place. He was just trying it out while Ursula wasn't around.
- Drew said he went to Ursula's to get his drumsticks, but when Max and Alison talked to him at his house they could see a set of drumsticks on the drums in his living room.
- When Ursula unlocked the side door for Andy, Max realized that it had been locked the whole time. Whoever blew out the amp had a key to the door and locked it on their way out, which means Kate couldn't have done it.
- Ursula said that her next-door neighbors, the Bacca family, had a set of keys for her house. That gave Drew access to Ursula's garage.
- Max and Alison noticed Andy still had his school uniform on when he came into the garage. He was just getting home–and didn't have his keys–so he couldn't have blown out the amp.
- Kate may have left Ursula's place in a hurry, but she wasn't fleeing the crime scene–she was going to get a new street hockey ball. Max noticed the packaging for the ball sitting next to her hockey net.

Conclusion

When Max and Alison presented their evidence to Drew, he apologized to Ursula and donated the entire contents of his piggy bank to get the amp fixed. After that, Ursula and her dad even taught him how to use it properly to avoid future blowouts!

THE CASE OF THE...
COMIC-CON CON

THE CASE OF THE... COMIC-CON CON

Strike two? Because Doug didn't show up on time, it looked like the organizers had given away his booth, too.

I didn't know where the presentation rooms were, so I went to the info booth. Someone with long black hair and a shirt that said "Staff" on the back told me they'd lead the way, and I followed. I was checking my phone and not really paying attention.

I walked into the room to find nothing but a basket of snacks and water. By the time I realized something was wrong, the doors had slammed closed behind me. I was in there for an hour!

Leslie is Doug's sister. He called her to ask for help after he realized he was locked in the room, but she was just getting to the hotel now. The trip should've taken her 15 minutes, but it took over an hour.

Travis runs the local comic shop, Manga Mania, and is the organizer of WMCAF. He was busy answering questions at the info booth, so he didn't have much to tell us, except that Doug disappeared very suddenly after checking in. When no one could find him, Travis assumed he got stage fright and left.

Kristoff Kane is the creator of *Daddy Long Legs*, our town's other cool arachnid-inspired comic. He already had booth space at the festival, but he took over Doug's and had no plans to give it back.

Crystal Diallo is president of our school's manga club. She told us that Doug and Tina created *Total Tarantula* together. Tina couldn't afford to help him get it printed, so he refused to give her any credit.

I found Tina's booth, but it took forever to get to the front of the line. It turned out that she didn't have money to help Doug with their comic because she had just paid to print her own 'zine.

TINA, YOU MUST REALLY WANT TO GET BACK AT DOUG FOR TAKING ALL THE CREDIT FOR *TOTAL TARANTULA*.

WHAT DOUG DID WAS UNCOOL. BUT SUCCESS IS THE BEST REVENGE, AND I'VE BEEN SELLING MY OWN STUFF ALL MORNING. I HAVEN'T EVEN TAKEN A BREAK!

Tina's Braina

Meanwhile, Alison was keeping an eye on Crystal. She caught her and Leslie talking anime—not conspiracy.

Alison and I met back up with Doug to share our info.

Do you know who conned Doug? All the clues are here. Turn the page for the solution.

THE CASE OF THE...

COMIC-CON CON

Who conned Doug?

Kristoff Kane. He locked Doug in the room to steal his table space and keep him from selling *Total Tarantula*.

Clues

- The long metal rod used to trap Doug was actually a leg from one of the tables on the festival floor. Max noticed that one of Kristoff's table legs was missing.
- The thank-you basket on Kristoff's table had Doug's name on it, but Kristoff's basket was missing. That's because Kristoff left his in the meeting room so Doug wouldn't get hungry or thirsty while trapped.
- Kristoff doesn't have long black hair, but his table was close to a stand selling black wigs. Alison even noticed a wig in the garbage.
- Doug said he was conned by someone wearing a shirt that said "Staff" on the back, but the actual staff shirts had the word on the front. That means the con artist was wearing a fake.
- Kristoff had all the materials to make a fake staff shirt and was actually wearing the fake underneath his collared shirt.
- Tina has long black hair, but she didn't have time to con Doug. She was busy at her table all morning.
- Alison thought it was suspicious that Leslie took so long to get to the festival to help Doug. But when she overheard Crystal and Leslie talking, she realized that Leslie was delayed because she was watching an anime TV show.

Conclusion

When Max and Alison presented their evidence, Kristoff confessed to trapping Doug in the room. He said he only planned to leave him in there for the morning and apologized for the crime. Travis gave Doug both of Kristoff's tables, and Doug ended up selling tons of comics. He then used some of the cash to buy a copy of Tina's 'zine.

THE CASE OF THE...

TOILET PAPER PRANK

THE CASE OF THE... TOILET PAPER PRANK

Max Finder, junior-high detective, here. A huge video game store was opening up in Whispering Meadows... right next to the Game Barn, our town's long-time gamer haven. Of course, Game Barn staffers John Chu and Deb Yay had mixed feelings about it: anger and outrage.

Ana Guzman was new in town. Her family was opening the game store. Until now, she'd been making friends and things had been going smoothly for her.

Blow over? More like blow *up*. That Friday night, someone covered the Guzmans' new house in toilet paper. Alison and I showed up early the next morning to find a lot of paper...and a lot of press.

Ana told us she saw John Chu in her neighborhood with a gym bag around 6:00, but she didn't know what he was doing there.

EVERYONE SAYS YOU GUYS ARE THE BEST DETECTIVES IN TOWN. WILL YOU TAKE THE CASE AND HELP ME FIGURE THIS OUT?

NO PROBLEM, ANA. WE'RE ALREADY ON THE JOB. IN FACT, OUR FORENSICS EXPERT SHOULD BE HERE ANY...

HEY, GUYS!

Zoe may be young, but examining crime scenes is in her blood. A few minutes later, she already had some info to share with us.

I WASN'T ABLE TO PULL ANY CLUES OFF THE TOILET PAPER ITSELF. I'VE TAKEN A SAMPLE AND I'LL GET A CLOSER LOOK BACK AT MY LAB. THAT SAID, I DID NOTICE SOMETHING STRANGE.

Getting fired wasn't going to stop us from chasing down the facts. We stopped by the Game Barn to talk to Deb. She and John were both working to pay for university and often pulled long hours at the store.

The Whispering Meadows Climbing Gym is a popular exercise spot. It's also a perfect training ground for anyone wanting to scale a house.

John climbed down and took off before we could get anything more out of him. But he left something behind that gave us a clue.
WEIRD. THAT GUY FORGOT HIS STUFF!

And with that, we were out of suspects. We tried to catch up with Ana at school on Monday, but Jessica Peeves held us off.
LEAVE HER ALONE, GUYS. I MEAN, SO WHAT IF THAT FLAGPOLE WITH THE TOILET PAPER WRAPPED AROUND IT IS RIGHT NEXT TO ANA'S WINDOW?

FUNNY TO SEE YOU TWO BEING SO FRIENDLY, JESSICA. RUMOR HAS IT THAT YOU'RE JEALOUS OF ANA'S NEWFOUND POPULARITY.
THAT'S SO NOT TRUE! IN FACT, MY FAMILY INVITED ANA'S OUT TO THE MOVIES THE NIGHT HER PLACE GOT TOILET PAPERED TO WELCOME THEM TO TOWN. IT WAS IN THE PAPER!
MAX! ALISON! YOU GUYS HAVE TO COME WITH ME!

Zoe took us to an empty science lab to fill us in on her toilet paper findings.
THIS IS NO ORDINARY TP, GUYS. UPON CLOSER INSPECTION, I NOTICED IT'S SILKINO BLUE!
SILKINO...?
IT'S THE WORLD'S GREENEST TOILET PAPER, MAX! NOT TO MENTION THE MOST EXPENSIVE!

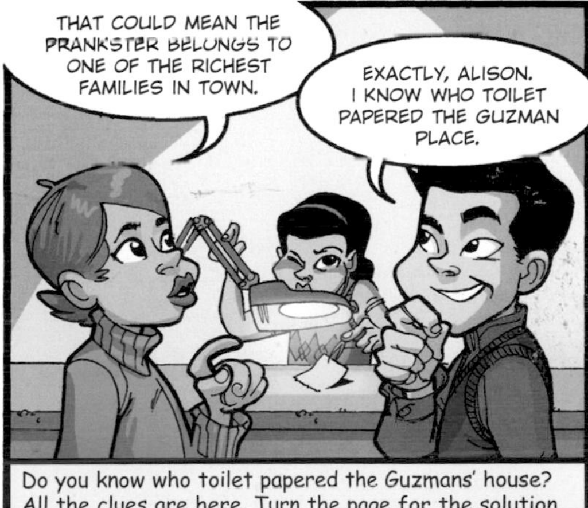

THAT COULD MEAN THE PRANKSTER BELONGS TO ONE OF THE RICHEST FAMILIES IN TOWN.
EXACTLY, ALISON. I KNOW WHO TOILET PAPERED THE GUZMAN PLACE.
Do you know who toilet papered the Guzmans' house? All the clues are here. Turn the page for the solution.

THE CASE OF THE...
TOILET PAPER PRANK

Who toilet papered the Guzmans' house?

Jessica Peeves. She was jealous of Ana and her status as the new girl in town.

Clues

- Jessica said her family took Ana's to the movies the night of the toilet papering, but the picture in the paper shows only Ana, her parents, and Jessica's parents.
- Because Ana and her family were at the movies, that meant none of them could have pulled the prank.
- Max and Alison saw John at the climbing gym, proving that he'd know how to scale a wall, but they also caught a glimpse of Jessica. She's a climber as well.
- Alison said the culprit belonged to one of the richest families in town. And as the newspaper said, Jessica's family is definitely one of the wealthiest.
- John may have been holding a bag near Ana's house, but that was at 6:00. As Alison said, the crime took place around 8:00.
- The bag John left at the climbing gym had the 1-Up Emporium logo on it. That's because he's their newest employee. Max pieced this together after they saw John's name crossed off the staff schedule at the Game Barn. John was in the Guzmans' neighborhood on the night of the toilet papering to accept the job. That's when he got the black gym bag.
- Deb wasn't lying when she said she was suddenly short staffed. The schedule said she worked until 9:00, which means she couldn't have committed the crime.

Conclusion

When Max and Alison confronted her with the Silkino Blue toilet paper, Jessica confessed to the crime. She apologized to Ana and her parents, and even showed up to support them at the opening of their new store–when it eventually opened across town from the Game Barn.

The Case of the Odd Job Shadow

As told by Max Finder

You know how Spider-Man has his spidey sense? Well, I have my mystery radar. It's the feeling I get when a mystery is about to present itself to me, and it's almost never wrong. It was an ordinary Tuesday morning, but my radar had been going off from the moment I woke up. It sat with me while I ate my breakfast cereal, chased me on my skateboard all the way to school, and was still there as I was grabbing books from my locker and getting ready to head to class.

So when I heard a small, squeaky voice calling my name from some unknown place in the halls, I wasn't so much surprised as confused. I recognized the voice, but it couldn't be...could it?

"Myron?" I asked, looking around. Out of a sea of passing classmates popped my eight-year-old next-door neighbor.

"Myron Matthews, reporting for duty, Mr. Finder!" he said joyously.

"I know who you are, Myron," I said. "What I don't know is what you're doing here!"

After some quick questioning, I got to the bottom of the strange visit. It turned out that everyone in Myron's third-grade class had to pick someone to shadow for a day to find out how jobs work in the real world. Myron chose me because he wants to be a detective, too.

"And your teacher let you do that?" I asked. "Job shadow me?"

"Well, I might have forgotten to tell her you're still in junior high school..." he said.

"Myron!" I shouted in exasperation. "Come on. We're heading to the office."

After talking with my school's principal and calling Myron's parents and teacher, I had a plan in place.

"Okay, here's the deal, Myron," I said. "At lunch I'm walking you across the park back to your school. In the meantime, you have to come to class with me. With any luck, it'll be a quiet morning."

"Something will happen, Mr. Finder! I just know it will," Myron said.

"You and me both," I muttered, my mystery radar still blaring.

Five, four, three, two, one...12:00 at last! The bell rang for lunch as I grabbed my math books from the desk, stuffed them into my bag, and pulled Myron out of the classroom as quickly as I could.

"Bye, Mr. Finder!" my classmates yelled after us, mimicking Myron's squeaky voice. Even Mr. Reed, my straight-faced math teacher, had to laugh at that one.

"Mr. Finder?" Myron said as I dragged him down the hall of the math and science wing, pretending not to hear him. "Mr. Finder, I have to go to the bathroom."

"Okay," I said, letting go of his T-shirt. I pointed him toward the bathroom just down the hall from where we were.

"When you're finished, I want you to meet me at my locker so we can..."

"Solve the mystery!" he said. "Got it!" And he ran off toward the bathroom.

"That's not what I meant!" I shouted, but he was already too far off. I headed back to my locker, unwrapped the tuna sandwich I'd packed for lunch, and ate it as quickly as humanly possible.

"Whoa, Max! What's the hurry?" my best friend, Alison Santos, said as she approached my locker.

I explained the whole morning: how Myron had lied to his teacher to be able to shadow me for a day, how everyone in all my morning classes thought that was hilarious, and how I wanted to get him back to his own school as soon as possible. A few minutes later I was finished with the story and my sandwich, but Alison wasn't sharing in my sense of outrage.

"Well, Max," she said, giggling, "it *is* kind of funny."

"Not you too!" I said.

"By the way, where is Myron?" she said.

Just then a strained, frantic voice called out "Max!" but it wasn't the voice I'd been expecting. It was Leslie Chang, our school's resident gossip, fashion queen, and talent show champ. Word had it that she'd been staying up late all month preparing a new dance routine for this year's show, and it was supposed to be awesome.

But right then she wasn't in the mood for bragging.

"Max!" she said as she ran up to us. "Someone stole my homework!"

As if we needed more excitement, Myron chose that moment to show up again.

"Mr. Finder! The soap dispenser exploded all over me," he said, stretching out his navy blue T-shirt to show us the sudsy mess. Our school had replaced the dispensers in both the boys' and girls' washrooms earlier that week, and they'd all been malfunctioning ever since. Anyone who wanted to wash their hands was getting sprayed with pink liquid soap—no exceptions.

"Oh, hello!" Myron said, noticing Leslie. "Do you have a case for Max Finder and Associates?"

"Myron!" I shouted.

"Oh, right!" he said, waving at Alison. "Finder, *Santos*, and Associates!"

"I think I'm going to like having Myron around!" Alison said, laughing.

"First of all, Myron isn't going to *be* around—he's going back to school right now. Second of all, I'm sorry, Leslie. Your homework problem is going to have to wait."

"It *can't* wait, Max!" Leslie wailed. "It's due this afternoon and I have no idea where it is. If I don't find it, I could get an F! If I get an F, I can't enter the talent show!"

Against my better judgment I agreed to drop by Leslie's locker on the way out of the school. It's in the middle of a long hallway. On one end is the area just outside the school's main office. On the other is the school's band room. It gets pretty quiet at lunch, making it the perfect hangout for our school's biggest bullies, Basher McGintley and his goons.

On the way over, Leslie told us she'd spent all night writing out a book report on *The Sisterhood of the Traveling Plants* by hand. She'd designed a cover on the computer, printed it out, and stapled the report together at home, stashing it in her book bag. She dropped by her locker at the start of lunch to drop off her book bag and then ran to the bathroom. When she returned, she realized she'd left her locker unlocked, and the report was gone.

"Who would want to steal someone's book report?" I mumbled to myself.

"Yes...who?" said Myron, who was standing right next to me. I looked over and noticed he was mimicking everything from my furrowed brow to the way I was crossing my arms and holding my hand under my chin.

"Stop it, Myron!"

"Yes, sir, Mr. Finder!" he said, snapping to military attention.

"If you guys are done playing Simon Says, I think I have an idea who might've done it," Leslie chimed in. "If I had to guess, I'd say it was Jessica Peeves."

Leslie told us that Jessica, the daughter of our town's mayor and one of the richest kids in school, was mad at her for also choosing to write about *Traveling Plants*. Apparently, Jessica chose it first.

"I didn't think it was such a big deal, but she always wants to be the only one to do things. Maybe she stole it to get back at me!" Leslie said.

That sure sounded like Jessica, and her locker was directly across the hall from Leslie's, but another thought was distracting me. What had taken Myron so long at the start of lunch? Was it possible he snuck off and stole the book report just so he could see me in action?

Deep in thought, I barely heard Alison talking to me.

"Earth to Max!" she said, and I snapped out of it. "I was just saying we should start by talking to some witnesses. Maybe someone saw something."

"Good idea, Alison," I said. "I think I know just where to start."

"Hey, Finder, who's the munchkin?" Basher shouted to the delight of his buddies as Myron and I drew close.

I was beginning to think it'd been a mistake to bring Myron along when he walked right up to Basher, struck his best tough-guy detective pose, and said, "Basher McGintley, I premuse."

"That's *presume*, Myron," I said, stepping between the two. "But yes, this is Basher, bully to the stars."

Then I turned my focus to the bully in question. Judging by the mess on his orange shirt, I thought he'd also fallen victim to the exploding soap dispenser earlier in the day. But then I figured it out: it was sloppy joe day in the cafeteria. Basher had the sticky orange fingers to prove it.

"Know anything about a stolen book report, Basher? Leslie's went missing from her locker a few minutes ago, and we all know you'd rather steal one than write one."

"Good point, Mr. Finder!" Myron said. "What do you say to that, Basher?"

"Whatever, Max. I don't know anything about Leslie's book report. What would I do with it? I'm not even in her class."

"Have you seen anybody hanging around her locker?"

"It's not like I've been keeping a lookout, but the only kid I've seen hanging around Leslie's locker is Leslie. Now take your talking Neopet and get lost!" he said, gesturing at Myron as he walked away.

To his credit, Myron completely ignored the insult Basher threw at him and focused on the case. Maybe there was a detective in there after all.

"I don't know, Mr. Finder," Myron said. "Basher doesn't make a very incredible witness."

"That's *credible* witness, Myron. But you're right. We need a lot more info and the clock is ticking...for Leslie and for us," I said. We still had to get Myron back to his school before lunch was over, or we were both in deep trouble.

With the sound of Basher's giggling still ringing in our ears, we walked back to Leslie's locker and found her in a frantic state. While she and Alison were standing around, Leslie had found the cover page to her essay lying on the ground.

"This was stapled to the rest of my report!" Leslie said as she handed the piece of paper to me. "It was right beside Jessica's locker, but Basher could've also dropped it on his way to the end of the hall."

I scanned the sheet for dead giveaways—like fingerprints or stains of any sort—but found nothing. I held the piece of paper out in front of me, right at Myron's eye level.

"Notice anything, Myron?" I asked.

"Looks just like a plain piece of computer paper, Mr. Finder," Myron said. "No rips or holes or anything."

"Thanks for stating the obvious, kid," Leslie said, picking a piece of lint off her crisp white polo shirt. "Maybe let the junior-high detectives handle this."

"Hang on, Leslie. I think Myron's on to something," I answered.

"I am?" Myron said, surprised.

"Yup. In fact, I think you just helped solve your first case. I know what happened to Leslie's homework."

Do you know who stole Leslie's homework?
Turn the page for the solution.

THE CASE OF THE... ODD JOB SHADOW

Who stole Leslie's book report?

Leslie Chang...kind of. She was busy practicing for the talent show and didn't have time to write her report, so she made up a story to make it look like the report had been stolen.

Clues

- Myron noticed that the cover page Leslie found had no rips or holes in it. That means it was never actually stapled to the rest of the book report. Leslie was lying.
- The report cover was nowhere to be found until Max and Myron went down the hall to talk to Basher. Leslie found it next to Jessica's locker because she planted it there to make Jessica or Basher look guilty.
- Leslie said she was in the bathroom when the book report was stolen, but unlike Myron, she didn't have a soapy mess on her shirt. Max described her shirt as crisp and white—not messy.
- Basher said the only kid he saw near Leslie's locker was Leslie. That means it couldn't have been Jessica.
- Max noticed that Basher had sticky orange fingers from eating sloppy joes. If he'd stolen the book report, the cover page Leslie picked up would've had his orange fingerprints all over it.
- Myron may have been missing at the time of the crime, but he was actually in the bathroom—he had soap on his shirt after the soap dispenser exploded on him. He also wouldn't have been able to go to the bathroom *and* steal the book report because there wasn't enough time—Leslie's locker and the bathroom are in different hallways.

Conclusion

When Max presented his evidence (and Myron shouted "Yeah!" every time he finished a sentence), Leslie confessed to making up the story. She said she was so into preparing her dance for the talent show that she forgot all about the book report. She got an F on the report and missed the show altogether, but she learned a valuable lesson: good dancers always do their homework!

THE CASE OF THE...

COPYCAT CRIME

THE CASE OF THE... COPYCAT CRIME

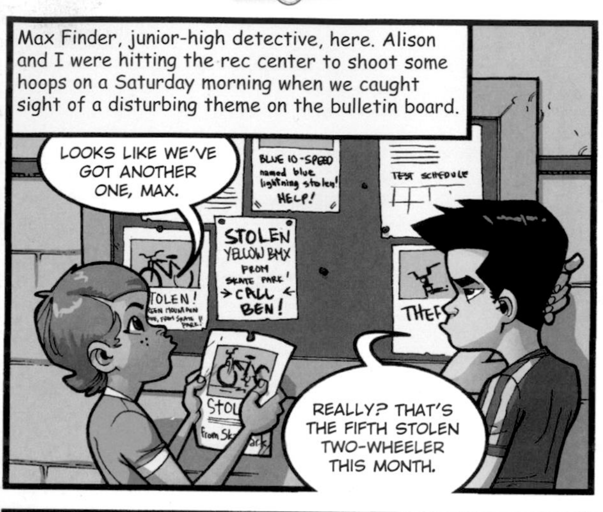

Ana Guzman is new in town. She showed up at the skate park to meet friends at around 10:00 a.m. Her bike vanished from the rack during the next half hour, but nobody at the park saw anything suspicious.

The bicycle bandit, a.k.a. Glen Edwards, is an infamous Whispering Meadows thief. He used a leaky car jack to break bike locks and then sold the bikes online. We tracked down Glen's address and tried to pay him a visit. Was he up to his old tricks?

With a suspect list the size of Whispering Meadows, we parted ways with Ana and headed to the skate park to track down eyewitnesses. We started with our classmate and skate park regular, Layne Jennings.

THIS THIEF ONLY STEALS FROM THE BIKE RACK IN THE SKATE PARK. YOU MUST HAVE SEEN SOMETHING STRANGE.

EVERYONE SITS ON THE OTHER SIDE OF THE SKATE PARK. EVERY TIME WE TURN OUR BACKS, A BIKE DISAPPEARS. PEOPLE ARE STARTING TO STAY AWAY.

WHO DO YOU TRUST, MAX?
LAYNE TOLD ME SHE'S BEEN LEARNING TO RIDE, BUT NATE THINKS IT'S NOT TRUE. IF SHE'S LYING ABOUT THAT, I WONDER WHAT ELSE SHE'D LIE ABOUT.

The next day, we decided to canvass the neighborhood to find out if anyone had seen anything suspicious. We were about to give up by the time we got to Mrs. Nelson's house.
I SEE SUSPICIOUS BEHAVIOR OVER THERE ALL THE TIME! KIDS ARE THERE FIRST THING IN THE MORNING, AND NOW THERE'S EVEN A BLOND GIRL WHO SKATES LATE INTO THE EVENING.
I WORK FROM HOME, AND THE NOISE IS AFFECTING MY CONCENTRATION!

DID YOU SEE ANYONE WHO MIGHT'VE STOLEN THE BIKES?
YOU KNOW, I DID SEE A BOY RIDING DOWN THE STREET YESTERDAY WITH A SKATEBOARD ACROSS HIS HANDLEBARS. I THOUGHT IT WAS PRETTY STRANGE.

IF I REMEMBER CORRECTLY, MRS. NELSON WAS ONE OF THE FEW PEOPLE WHO SPOKE OUT AGAINST THE SKATE PARK BEFORE IT GOT BUILT. SHE'S NEVER BEEN A FAN OF HAVING IT IN HER NEIGHBORHOOD.
GOOD POINT, BUT—HEY, ISN'T THAT FELIX'S BIKE FROM THE FLYER? BASHER...WAIT!
EAT DUST, FINDER!
GINGERBREAD AND BISCUITS

HE'LL HAVE TO DOUBLE BACK TO GET HOME. LET'S HEAD HIM OFF!

Ben "Basher" McGintley may be the biggest bully in the history of Whispering Meadows, but he's not quick enough to get past Alison.
WHOA!
NICE BIKE, BASHER! MIND TELLING US WHERE YOU GOT IT?
I'M NOT TELLING YOU ANYTHING!

FINE. THEN YOU CAN JUST TALK TO EVERYONE ELSE WHEN WE TELL THEM YOU'RE THE NEW BICYCLE BANDIT...
THE NEW WHAT? NO WAY! I FOUND THIS BIKE IN THE WOODS BEHIND THE SKATE PARK LAST MONTH. I JUST FIGURED SOMEONE DITCHED IT. YOU CAN HAVE IT.

After telling Basher not to leave town, we grabbed Zoe, our friend and forensics expert, and headed to the woods.
THE BIKES ARE DIRTY, BUT THEY'RE ALL HERE IN ONE PIECE.
DETECTIVES AT WORK

LOOKS LIKE SEVERAL OF THESE GOT THE OIL TREATMENT AS WELL.
WHAT OIL? THIS SUBSTANCE LOOKS LIKE MOLASSES. MY MOM USES IT FOR BAKING.

NICE CATCH, ZOE. I HAVE A FEELING THIS STICKY STUFF IS GOING TO PUT SOMEONE IN A STICKY SITUATION.
ME, TOO. I KNOW WHO'S BEEN STEALING THE BIKES.
Do you know who stole the bikes? All the clues are here. Turn the page for the solution.

THE CASE OF THE...
COPYCAT CRIME

Who stole the bikes?

Mrs. Nelson. She hid the bikes in the woods in order to scare kids away from the park so she could work from home in peace. She used molasses to make Max and Alison think the original bicycle bandit was up to his old tricks again.

Clues

- Mrs. Nelson lives across the street from the skate park, so she knew exactly when the skaters were distracted and bikes were vulnerable. Max even noticed a telescope in her front window pointed at ground level. She used it to watch the skate park.
- Mrs. Nelson said she works from home. That gives her lots of time to steal bikes.
- Layne told Max she was learning to ride, and she was–but not when Nate could see her. Mrs. Nelson said a blond girl was riding late at night. It was Layne. She didn't want Nate complaining about her, so she waited until after he'd left the park to practice.
- When Mrs. Nelson said she saw a boy riding down the street with a skateboard across his handlebars, she was lying. Layne said she saw Nate leaving the park that day on his skateboard.
- Nate may have been using oil to tune up his skateboard, but he didn't use it in connection with stealing any bikes. As Zoe said, the "oil" Max and Alison saw was actually molasses.
- As the delivery truck parked in her driveway suggested, Mrs. Nelson is a baker, and that's why she had so much molasses on hand.

Conclusion

When Max and Alison presented their evidence, Mrs. Nelson confessed. She explained that she never intended to keep the bikes hidden forever. Because the bikes were all returned unscathed, the courts went easy on Mrs. Nelson. She was sentenced to 50 days of volunteer work...raising money for new skate park features!

THE CASE OF THE...

BIRTHDAY PARTY TREACHERY

THE CASE OF THE...
BIRTHDAY PARTY TREACHERY

Max Finder, junior-high detective, here. It was a Saturday morning on the opening weekend of *Tailor Spoon: Spoonful of Hearts*. Crystal Diallo had rented out our local theater to screen the movie for her birthday, and Alison and I were helping set up.

We tried calling the number, but no one answered, so Alison started looking it up on the 'net. Then things went from bad to worse as Trina, the manager of the theater, arrived for her shift.

Nicole Pilton is one of our town's premier princesses. When we asked her to let Crystal have the theater back, she wouldn't give us the time of day.

James Tiberius goes to our school. He's friends with Crystal and has played hockey with Tony forever, but early on he decided to go to Crystal's birthday party.

By the time Alison and I made it to Tony's house, we had only 90 minutes left on the clock. We went straight to T. DeMatteo himself.

On our way out, we bumped into Dorothy Pafko. She's helped us with lots of cases in the past, and had some info to share when we told her what we'd been up to.

I'M AMAZED TONY WOULD LET GO OF HIS CELL PHONE FOR EVEN A MINUTE! HE'S BEEN GLUED TO IT ALL MORNING AND IGNORING HIS GUESTS.

DID YOU SEE ANYTHING ELSE SUSPICIOUS AROUND HERE?

JUST A LITTLE GRUMBLING. LOTS OF KIDS FELT CAUGHT IN THE MIDDLE OF THE TWO PARTIES TONIGHT, BUT I GUESS THAT'S NOT A PROBLEM NOW.

TOO BAD, THOUGH. I REALLY WANTED TO SEE THAT TAILOR SPOON MOVIE!

With Alison off on her mysterious mission, I raced back downtown. On the way there, I ran into James headed home to change for Tony's bowling party.

Thanks to my chat with James, Alison and I made it back to the theater at the exact same time. I told her what James had said, and she caught me up on her mystery trip.

Do you know who tried to cancel Crystal's party? All the clues are here. Turn the page for the solution.

THE CASE OF THE... BIRTHDAY PARTY TREACHERY

Who sent the fake text?

James Tiberius. He is friends with both Crystal and Tony and felt caught in the middle, so he used Phil's cell phone to send the bogus text to get Crystal's party canceled.

Clues

- When James first ran into the theater, he told Crystal he got the "fake text," but nobody had told him that it was fake yet. He was lying. He also told Max later on that he doesn't even have a cell phone.
- James had blueberry stains on his teeth—they were exactly like the kind Dorothy had on her teeth at Tony's brunch. That means James was at the DeMatteo place that morning.
- When Phil got to the brunch after hockey practice, he found his cell phone on a table just inside the front door. It was in the house the whole time he was gone, so James had lots of time to place the text.
- Dorothy said Tony was glued to his phone all morning, but there are two reasons for that. First, it was his birthday present. Second, as Alison noted when he handed it over, he was using it to look up hockey scores.
- Nicole called Crystal "Krista" at the movie theater. That means she didn't even know Crystal's name, let alone who was on her party guest list or their phone numbers. She couldn't have placed the text.

Conclusion

When Max and Alison presented their evidence, Crystal called James at home and got him to confess. Nicole took back her reservation, and both Crystal and Tony's parties went off without a hitch. The two groups were able to meet up for ice cream later that night, and Crystal and Tony agreed to host joint parties from then on!

THE CASE OF THE...

DAYDREAMING DETECTIVE

THE CASE OF THE... DAYDREAMING DETECTIVE

MS. CHANG
BY SUN-TIMES REPORTER ALISON SANTOS
A LAVISH POOL PARTY ENDED
IN EXCITEMENT AND CONFUSION
LAST NIGHT AS A PRICELESS
PIECE OF JEWELRY WENT MISSING FROM A
WHISPERING MEADOWS HOME. THE JEWELRY
IN QUESTION IS MALTA'S FAMOUS FALCONI
EARRINGS, A PIECE THAT HAD ONLY RECE
COME INTO THE POSESSION OF LOCAL MIL-
LIONAIRE MS. SASHA PRICE. SINGING SEN
TION LESLIE CHANG, SEEN RUNNING FROM
SCENE OF THE CRIME, IS WANTED FOR QU
TIONING, BUT WAS UNAVAILABLE FOR COM
NICE WRITING, SANTOS. WHERE CAN WE FIND MS. CHANG?
DIDN'T YOU READ THE STORY? SHE'S ON THE RUN! WHAT DO YOU THINK, SHE'S JUST GOING TO WALK IN HERE AND...

SLAM
MR. FINDER! YOU'VE GOTTA HELP ME!
YOU WERE SAYING, SANTOS?

After a few minutes, Ms. Chang calmed down enough to talk to us.
I KNOW IT LOOKS BAD, BUT I DIDN'T STEAL THOSE EARRINGS.
BLUB
BLUB
TELL US WHAT HAPPENED, AND START FROM THE BEGINNING.

As soon as I got to the party, Sasha Price started going on about the earrings. She was talking so loudly everyone could hear her.
YOU HAVE TO SEE THEM! THEY'RE WORTH MORE THAN YOUR HOUSE!

I went to the back bedroom to check them out, but the earrings were gone. I heard Sasha coming and I panicked. I took off out the patio doors!
HEY!

INTERESTING TALE. HOW DO WE KNOW YOU'RE TELLING THE TRUTH?
YOU TELL ME. IF I WAS IN THE POSSESSION OF PRICELESS EARRINGS, DO YOU THINK I'D BE HANGING AROUND HERE?

We left Ms. Chang and headed over to the crime scene to talk to Sasha Price, who seemed to be in mourning.
PARDON ME FOR SAYING SO, MS. PRICE, BUT YOU SEEM TO BE TAKING THIS PRETTY HARD.
OF COURSE! FINALLY I GET MY HANDS ON A TRULY ONE-OF-A-KIND ITEM AND THEN IT'S TAKEN AWAY.

I'D BEEN TAKING CALLS NONSTOP FROM COLLECTORS WHO WANTED TO BUY THE EARRINGS. NOW THE ONLY PEOPLE I HEAR FROM ARE INSURANCE AGENTS.

Could Ms. Price have stolen the earrings herself to claim the insurance money? I pondered this as we came across crime scene investigator Zoe Palgrave.
I FOUND THIS HIDDEN IN THE RUG. MS. PRICE SAYS SHE'S NEVER SEEN IT BEFORE.
COULD BE THE CALLING CARD OF THE THIEF.
AND THAT'S NOT ALL...

THE LOCK ON THE PATIO DOORS IS BROKEN. LOOKS LIKE IT HAS BEEN FOR SOME TIME.
THAT MEANS THE PARTY COULD HAVE HAD AN UNINVITED GUEST OR TWO.
LIKE WHO?

LIKE *HIM!*
THAT'S NICHOLAS MUSICCO! HE AND HIS FAMILY HAVE BEEN FEUDING WITH THE PRICES FOR YEARS!

A quick scan of the party photos found Mr. Musicco in attendance, but he wasn't on the guest list and no one saw him leave. We visited him at his home.

Spodek was playing that night, so we hit the ballpark to check up on Musicco's story.

BRRRRRRING!

MAX? HOW WAS YOUR ALL-NIGHTER? ANY NEW THOUGHTS ON THE CASE?
ALISON! NO... UH, MAYBE! I FELL ASLEEP, BUT I'VE GOT A HUNCH. MEET ME AT SASHA'S PLACE.

Just as in my dream, we found Sasha lounging by the pool.
WHEN THE GUESTS WERE LEAVING YOUR PARTY, DID YOU CONDUCT A SEARCH FOR THE EARRINGS?
OF COURSE! I HAD MY BUTLER CHECK EVERYONE'S POCKETS. I EVEN HAD HIM INSPECT THE EARLOBES OF EVERY GIRL AT THE PARTY!

THAT DOESN'T RULE OUT ANYONE WHO LEFT EARLY. NICHOLAS COULD'VE POCKETED THEM.
LESLIE COULD'VE, TOO!
HOLD UP, GUYS. I'M READY TO END THIS GUESSING GAME. I KNOW WHO STOLE THE EARRINGS.
Do you know who took Sasha's earrings? All the clues are here. Turn the page for the solution.

THE CASE OF THE... DAYDREAMING DETECTIVE

Who stole Sasha Price's earrings?

Josh Spodek. He overheard Sasha telling Leslie about the earrings, and he stole them so he could make a profit.

Clues

- Alison noticed Josh signing his number, 23, on an autograph at the ballpark. That matches up with the number on the pin Zoe found on the floor at the crime scene. The pin was actually Josh's earring—he dropped it when he stole Malta's Falconi earrings from Sasha's bedroom.
- Max noticed a glare around Josh's left ear in the party photo of him and Nicholas. It was the flash reflecting off one of the earrings. Max figured this out at the ballpark later when he saw that Josh has his ears pierced.
- Sasha said she had everyone's pockets and the earlobes of every girl checked before anyone could leave, but she didn't say anything about the boys' earlobes. That explains how Josh was able to walk out of the party with the earrings.
- Josh said he didn't see Nicholas at Sasha's party, but in the photo of the two of them Nicholas is clearly reaching out to tap him on the shoulder. Josh was lying to make Nicholas look guilty.
- Alison knew Sasha wouldn't have stolen the earrings for insurance money. She clearly cared more about attention than money—which she has quite enough of as it is!

Conclusion

When Max and Alison showed Josh the "23" earring Zoe found on the floor of the crime scene, he confessed. He returned Malta's Falconi earrings to Sasha, who agreed not to press charges, and apologized for all the trouble he'd caused. He also resolved to find another way to make money—after he stops being grounded, of course!

HOST YOUR OWN MYSTERY PARTY
SHHH! HERE'S HOW...

SETTING UP

1. Pick out your favorite Max Finder Mystery—try to find one that has the number of people in it that you want to invite to your party, including yourself.

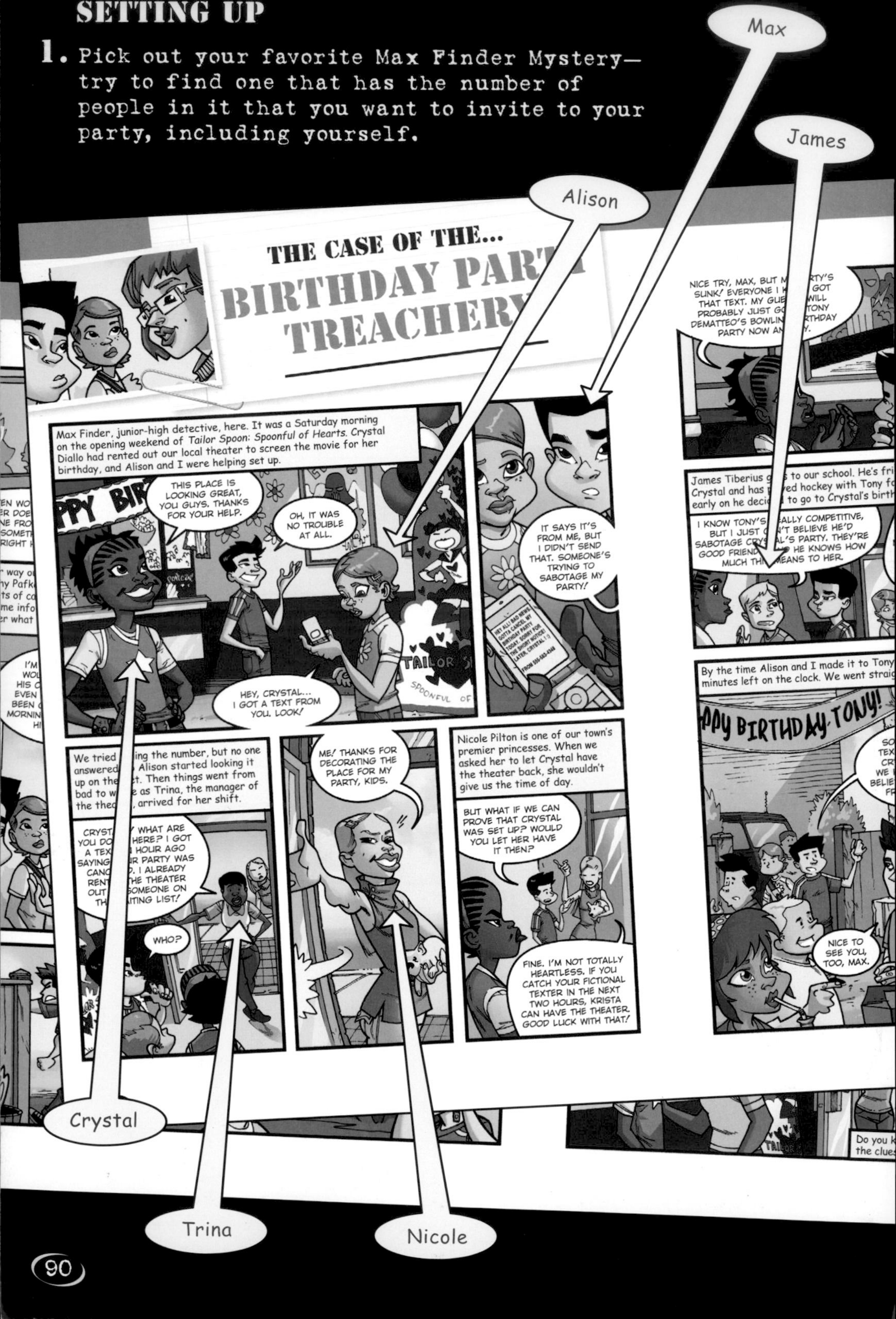

2. Assign a character to each guest—make yourself Max or Alison, since you'll be the host of the party and they're the main narrators of the comics! Write out a little description of each role (personality, favorite clubs or sports, that kind of thing) on a card so that the guests will be able to get into character right away.

CRYSTAL: character profile

She is a girl who is usually found reading or drawing but is outside a lot because she is a dog walker. She likes to wear bright colors—to match her personality!

The Case of the Birthday Party Treachery

MAX INTRO VOICE-OVER
Max Finder, junior-high detective, here. It was a Saturday morning on the opening weekend of ***Tailor Spoon: Spoonful of Hearts***. Crystal Diallo had rented out our local theater to screen the movie for her birthday, and Alison and I were helping set up.

CRYSTAL: This place is looking great, you guys. Thanks for your help!

MAX: Oh, it was no trouble at all.

ALISON: Hey, Crystal...I got a text from you. Look!

TEXT READS: HEY ALL! BAD NEWS. GOTTA CANCEL MY BIRTHDAY PARTY TODAY. SORRY FOR THE SHORT NOTICE! LATER, CRYSTAL! :)

CRYSTAL: It says it's from me, but I didn't send that. Someone's trying to sabotage my party!

MAX VOICE-OVER
We tried calling the number, but no one answered, so Alison started looking it up on the 'net. Then things went from bad to worse as Trina, the manager of the theater, arrived for her shift.

TRINA: Crystal?! What are you doing here? I got a text an hour ago saying your party was canceled. I already rented the theater out to someone on the waiting list!

MAX: Who?

NICOLE: Me! Thanks for decorating the place for my party, kids.

One of the most important traits of a good detective is being able to make observations and get into the heads of your suspects.

3. Type up or write out a script of the case you want to solve—be sure to make enough copies so that each guest has one to read from. But make sure you don't include the solution to the case!

4. Identify any key props you'll need for the case you want to solve. Will you need a skateboard? Some rolls of toilet paper? How about a pretend yearbook with all your guests' faces in it?

This is a great way to reuse old magazines, photos, and cardboard that you have kicking around. Find what you can around the house or borrow from a neighbor, and get crafty for the rest—just check with an adult before using anything someone might miss!

What's a crime without physical evidence to look at? Unsolved, that's what! You'll need to create props so your friends can make conclusions on their own and capture the culprit!

5. When your guests arrive, give them their scripts and props and about fifteen minutes to read over their lines and get a feel for their characters. Give everyone a small notepad and pen to keep track of clues and possible suspects.

6. Pick a spot in your house or outside that fits the mood of the crime scene—you can decorate to enhance this! (For example, make a pretend popcorn stand for "The Case of the Birthday Party Treachery" and hand out mini paper bags full of popcorn to help your guests really get into the scene.)

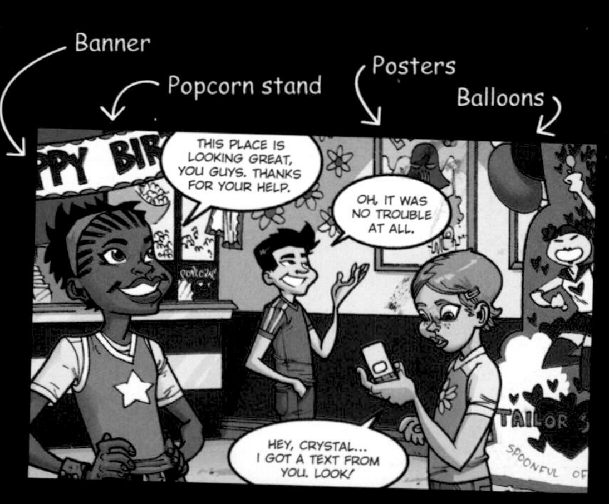

7. Start acting!

Take turns saying your lines according to the script.